Dear Parent:

Here's something new: a picture book which shows an adult who needs help.

Whether it's helping to tie a shoe or answering a difficult question about arithmetic, adults usually are on the helping end. In *Mrs. Toggle's Zipper*, her students arrive in their classroom and find Mrs. Toggle looking upset because she can't get her coat undone. First the school nurse tries to help, then the principal, and finally, the custodian, Mr. Abel, finds a common sense solution. In the context of this amusing story, children learn that their teacher is just as human as they are and that everyone needs help sometimes.

Already *Mrs. Toggle's Zipper* has received high scores. *Booklist* said: "A great choice as a read-aloud for an entire class or a read-alone for a private giggle." *Kirkus* said: "A winner." We hope you and your children will enjoy it, too.

Sincerely,

Stephen Fraser

Stephen Fraser
Senior Editor
Weekly Reader Book Club

MRS. TOGGLE'S ZIPPER

Weekly Reader Children's Book Club Presents

MRS. TOGGLE'S ZIPPER

Robin Pulver

Illustrated by R. W. Alley

Four Winds Press   New York

For Nina, who started it all—R.P.

For Isaac, Sherri, and Meggie—R.W.A.

This book is a presentation of Newfield Publications, Inc.
Newfield Publications offers book clubs for children from preschool through high school.
For further information write to: **Newfield Publications, Inc.,**
4343 Equity Drive, Columbus, Ohio 43228.

Published by arrangement with Four Winds Press, an imprint of Macmillan Publishing Company, a division of Macmillan, Inc.
Newfield Publications is a trademark of Newfield Publications, Inc. Weekly Reader is a federally registered trademark
of Weekly Reader Corporation.

Printed in the United States of America.

Library of Congress Cataloging-in-Publication Data • Pulver, Robin. Mrs. Toggle's Zipper/Robin Pulver;
illustrated by R. W. Alley—1st ed. p cm. Summary: When Mrs. Toggle's zipper sticks and traps her inside her coat,
everyone in the school tries to free her but with little success.
ISBN 0-02-775451-0
[I. Zippers—Fiction. 2. Schools—Fiction. 3. Humorous stories.]
I. Alley, R.W. (Robert W.), ill. II. Title. III. Title: Missus Toggle's zipper.
PZ7.P97325Mr 1990 [E]—dc19 88-37251 CIP AC

When Mrs. Toggle's children arrived at school in the morning, they changed in the hall from their boots to their shoes.

When the bell rang, they picked up their boots and book bags and marched along to their room.

They stuffed boots and bags into their cubbyholes and hung up their coats. Then they sat down at their desks.

"Good morning, Mrs. Toggle," the children said in their best morning voices.

"Good morning, class," said Mrs. Toggle in an unusually grumpy voice.

Then the children noticed that Mrs. Toggle was still wearing her coat—the big, puffy, fuchsia-colored one that she got for Christmas.

"Mrs. Toggle!" yelled Joey. "You forgot to take off your coat!"

"I didn't forget," said Mrs. Toggle uncomfortably. "I can't take it off because the zipper is stuck. I'm afraid it's going to be a long, hot day."

"How'd the zipper get stuck?" Nina asked.

Mrs. Toggle fanned her face. "How does any zipper get stuck? First a tiny bit of cloth gets caught in it. Then you pull and keep pulling a little too hard. And before you know it, you're trapped in your coat like a hand in a cookie jar."

The children gathered around Mrs. Toggle's desk to see for themselves.

"Yup," said Joey, "that zipper sure *is* stuck." The others nodded.

"What's worse," said Mrs. Toggle, "the thingamajig is gone."

"The what?" said the children.

"The thingamajig—that you pull the zipper up and down with. Mine is lost."

"Oh," groaned the children. They all thought happily about their own coats hanging on hooks with their zippers open and the thingamajigs still on them.

"Maybe we can help," said Caroline.

"It's worth a try," said Mrs. Toggle.

Mrs. Toggle braced her feet on the floor. She leaned forward in her chair and held out her arms. Some children grabbed one sleeve; some, the other sleeve. Paul and Nina grabbed fistfuls of collar.

"Now!" yelled Mrs. Toggle, and everybody pulled.

And everybody landed, with thuds and bumps, in a heap on the floor. Mrs. Toggle's collar was as far as her nose, but no further than that.

Paul wanted to get busy learning the times tables. "Mrs. Toggle," he said, "let's go to the nurse's office. Maybe Mrs. Schott can help you."

So Mrs. Toggle and the children trudged down to the office of Mrs. Schott, the school nurse.

When Mrs. Schott saw Mrs. Toggle's hot, red face, she reached for the thermometer and popped it into Mrs. Toggle's mouth.

Mrs. Toggle shook her head. "Addon avva tepashhur!"

"Don't talk with a thermometer in your mouth," said Mrs. Schott sternly. "I'll telephone your mother."

"Addon livwif ma mudder," mumbled Mrs. Toggle.

"Mouth closed!" ordered Mrs. Schott.

Nina spoke up. "She's not sick, and she doesn't live with her mother because she's a grown-up. Mrs. Toggle is hot because she can't get her coat off. The zipper's stuck, and the thingamajig is lost."

"Then we must pull it off," said Mrs. Schott.

"Oh, we tried that," Paul said.

"This time we'll add a bandage," the nurse answered. "Bandages make boo-boos better. But first, Mrs. Toggle, you must take that thermometer out of your mouth!"

Mrs. Schott stuck a bandage on the zipper where the thingamajig was supposed to be. Then she pulled, and the children pulled, and they all ended up with thuds, bumps, and bangs on the floor of Mrs. Schott's office.

Mrs. Toggle's collar was as far as her nose, but no further than that.

Mrs. Schott shook her head. "I must call the principal. He'll know what to do with you."

The principal, Mr. Stickler, left important matters on his desk to hurry to the nurse's office.

Mr. Stickler frowned when he saw Mrs. Toggle. "Mrs. Toggle, it's against school rules to wear your coat all day."

"I am sorry," said Mrs. Toggle, "but I can't take my coat off. The zipper is stuck."

"Tell him about the thingamajig!" said Nina.

"The what?" Mr. Stickler asked.

"You know," said Paul, "the whatsit."

"The doodad," said Caroline.

"The whatchamacallit," said Joey.

"My students are right," said Mrs. Toggle. "The thingamajig is missing from my zipper."

The principal frowned again. "Mrs. Toggle," he said, "in my job I have learned that if you want to get out of a tight spot, you must follow the rules.

"Pay attention, children," he said. "Make two straight lines. One line pull on the right arm, the other line pull on the left. Mrs. Schott, you be responsible for the collar. I shall pull on Mrs. Toggle's feet."

"We've tried that," said Joey.

"Pulling doesn't work," Nina agreed.

"Did you make straight lines?" asked Mr. Stickler. "That's the rule. Stay in straight lines. Now, get ready...get set...pull!"

The children and Mrs. Schott pulled in one direction.
Mr. Stickler pulled in the other direction. Mrs. Toggle tried to
make herself small and wriggly. But with thuds, bumps, bangs,
and a kerplop, they all ended up on the floor once more.

Mrs. Toggle's collar was as far as her nose, but no
further than that.

Mr. Stickler said, "Enough of this. We don't want holes in the school floor just because of Mrs. Toggle's zipper. I'm calling the custodian. I'm afraid he'll have to cut this coat off!"

"No!" yelled the children, and Mrs. Toggle cried, "Never!"

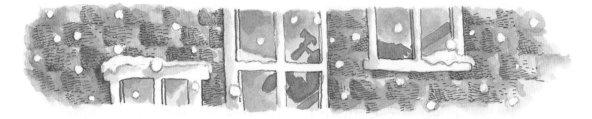

The custodian, Mr. Abel, arrived wearing his big work apron. Tools bulged in every pocket. He looked at Mrs. Toggle in her coat. "Is the building too cold for you?" he asked kindly. "Maybe the thermostat's off. I'll go check."

"Wait!" said Mr. Stickler.

"See," said Caroline, "Mrs. Toggle can't get her coat off because the zipper's stuck."

"Yes," the principal said, "and there's a problem with the thingamajig."

Mr. Abel listened carefully. "Mmm," he said. "I can see the pull-tab is gone."

"The what?" said the children and Mrs. Toggle and the nurse and the principal all together.

"I said, the pull-tab's gone. Don't worry, I've seen worse."

Mr. Abel pulled a pair of needle-nose pliers out of one huge apron pocket. He used the pliers to loosen the grip of the zipper's metal teeth on the shiny, fuchsia-colored lining of Mrs. Toggle's coat.

Gently, with his large fingers, Mr. Abel eased the lining away from the teeth. Then he slid the zipper down, down, down. It opened completely. Mr. Abel helped Mrs. Toggle off with her coat.

A happy smile spread over Mrs. Toggle's face. Mrs. Schott and Mr. Stickler and the children cheered.

"You should get a new pull-tab for that zipper before you zip it up again," said the custodian.

"I surely will, Mr. Abel," said Mrs. Toggle. "I am forever grateful to you."

The principal went back to important matters. Mrs. Schott rushed off to check a child for chicken pox. Mrs. Toggle and the children traipsed back to their room to tackle the times tables.

Mr. Abel pulled a small pad from his huge apron pocket and wrote himself a reminder: "Remember to look up 'thingamajig' in the dictionary."